Can you keep a secret?
Promise not to tell, 'cause
this is a BIG secret.
First here's the crew of
the Night Brigade:

there's
Number 1,
the Captain...

...Number 2,
the Deputy...

...Number 3,
the
Navigator...

...Number 4,
the
Mechanic...

.Number 5,
the
Muscle...

...Number 6,
the
Timekeeper...

...and me. I'm Number 7,
and I joined the Night
Brigade on Tuesday.
I'm the new kid.

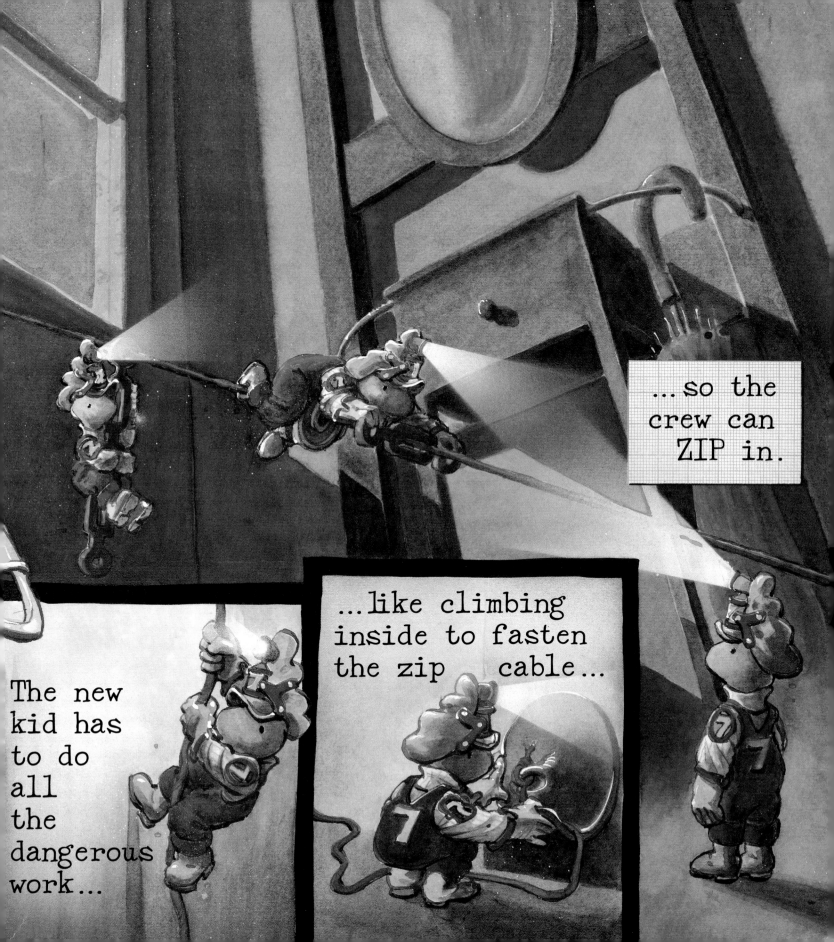

...and we're off.

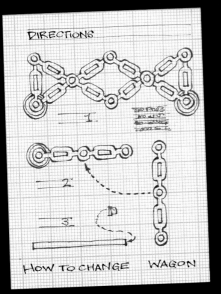

DIRECTIONS

1.

2.

3.

HOW TO CHANGE WAGON

When we
get to the
big furry
cliffs, we
change the
wagon

into
the
cliff-climber.

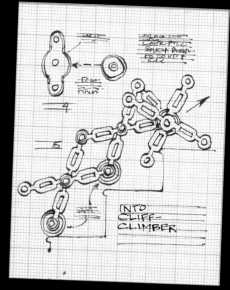

It's a tough climb, but we always make it to the top. Now we all go dead quiet, because here's where the real action starts.

SHHH.

We're going into...

...The Slumber Zone.

In the Slumber Zone, the crew work together like well-oiled machinery...

...or ELSE.

Make a mistake in the <u>Zone</u>, and you're <u>squashed</u>.

The suction cup sticks on here.

They use a candle to make hot air.

Wow!

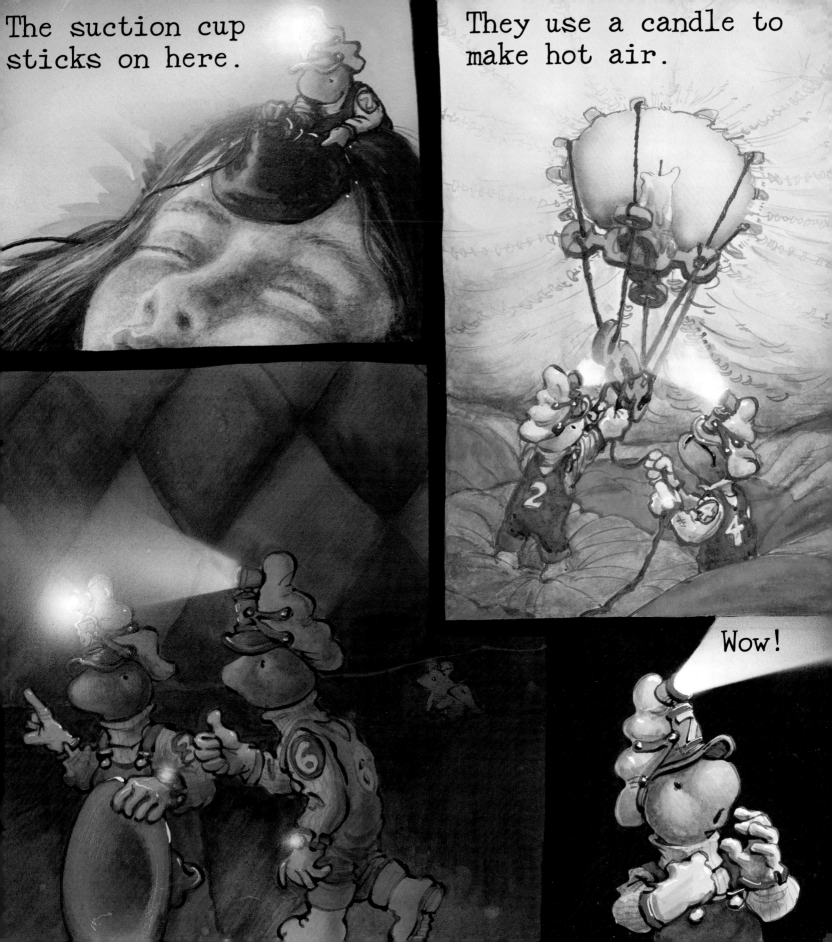

It floats!

...The Sky Buggy.

DIVIDED WE FALL! YO!

Remember, you <u>promised</u> to keep
our Mission a secret, so don't
tell anyone else, not even your
teddy bear. And the tooth? Sorry,
but we're not allowed to tell <u>anybody</u>
what we do with all the teeth...
not even <u>you</u>...

...it's TOP SECRET.

Scholastic Children's Books,
Commonwealth House, 1-19 New Oxford Street,
London WC1A 1NU, UK
a division of Scholastic Ltd
London ~ New York ~ Toronto ~ Sydney ~ Auckland

First published in hardback by Scholastic Ltd, 1996
This edition published by Hippo, an imprint of Scholastic Ltd, 1998

Text, illustrations and Typotoon typeface copyright © Ted Dewan, 1996

ISBN 0 590 19806 8

Printed in Hong Kong

For Helen